FAREWELL

Olivia's Seventh Wish

Daphne Dennis

Copyright

Social Stamina – 1,2,3 Let's Go!

Titles to help look at things from other perspectives and strengthen your mindset.

The Great Ascension–1,2,3 Let's Go!

Titles to help you gain focus and climb the ladder of success!

How to Start – 1,2,3 Let's Go!

Titles to help you with step-by-step, must-have knowledge of the business world and personal experiences.

Top 10 Questions to Ask Before You…1,2,3 Let's Go!

Titles with must-have questions (and logic behind) for many of life's daily and major decisions.

Find our fiction below!

https://www.ttpublishinghouse.com/legendsreborn

https://www.ttpublishinghouse.com/7wishes

https://www.ttpublishinghouse.com/mallcadet

Social Media

Facebook: tlmpublishinghouse

Website: www.TTpublishinghouse.com

Want to Read for Free?

You may qualify for a spot on our Advance Reader Copy group.

Never heard of an ARC Group?

Simply put, it's a small group of people who are interested in a specific genre and are invited to read books before they're published.

Your feedback can help alter the storyline or even catch an elusive typo!

You're asked to provide an honest review when it is published, and that's it!

You read for free!

Go now to confirm your interest in the ARC Group!
https://www.ttpublishinghouse.com/joinTLMarc

CONTENTS

THE MORNING AFTER

I open my eyes slowly; the bright early morning sunlight flittering in through the window makes me squint; I close my eyes again and mentally prepare myself this time, and then I open my eyes fully. Automatically, my brain starts to analyze where I am; I run my hand over the soft bed and slowly turn on my back. I still have no idea where I am, but I realize I feel happy. Huh. I look around the room and, seeing the grey sofa where I remember we had flung the condom wrapper and then the bedside lamp, which is now off, but yesterday was on and flooded the room with the ambiance that was the background of our lovemaking, and Cade's left slipper on the floor by the door, makes my body go warm. The memories of being with Cade start to assail me; the way his hands trailed lightly over my body, the tingles I felt running down my arm, the very intense look in his eyes the whole time, the words he whispered in my ears- before Cade, I never even knew that was a thing I would be interested in, well turns out I am very interested- last night was one of the best nights of my life.

And the wonderful feeling would have spilled into today if not for Cade's words yesterday, just before we fell asleep. He wondered what it would have been like if we hadn't met each other, like, 'imagine if your car hadn't broken down, and I hadn't come around.' Well, I don't have to imagine; I wished for the whole thing.

I bury my face in my pillow and let out a frustrated grunt into it. God, knowing the truth behind our meeting is like this big grey cloud full of doom, ready to burst open any day now, over my head. Speaking of, where is Cade? I sit up on the bed and look around; my eyes come to rest on a folded piece of paper on the bedside table. I can feel my lips already twitching. I open the folded paper and read what Cade wrote there; *Apparently, this hotel doesn't know how much you love chicken wings, even in the mornings, because they are out of them. Can you believe that?! Anyway, I have gone to get you some, even if I have to fly a helicopter to Africa, I will get those wings to you. Wait prettily. Cade.*

God, I love him! I crumple the paper to my face for a minute, and then I lift my face up, and a huge grin spreads on my face like a fool. Cade. He makes me feel things I had never felt before, things I never ever thought I would feel. I put the paper on my lap and start straightening the creases out of it with my hands. Now that I am actually in love, I feel pity for the women who aren't, who have never been. It is a wonderful feeling, no, better than that; it is ethereal. Right now, sitting on this hotel bed in nothing but my bra and panties, smoothening a BRB letter- that feels like a love letter- on my lap, I feel like I can do anything. Like, I feel down for literally anything. I can feel my body humming with happiness, all my nerves are alive, and the world is just beautiful; there is no sadness, just happiness, no death, only life, no difficult choices; only beautiful, easy ones. But in the corner of my mind, I know it isn't, and I know all I have to do is step out of this room and into the real world, and I would see it all, but, nonetheless, all I feel is happiness.

"Ugh, did you swallow a rainbow?" Clive says, his tone full of irritation. I look at him sitting on the bedside table, and he gives me a sour look, "Will you quit smiling already? You're scaring the bejesus out of me, looking all creepy with that insane smile on your face," he says when I keep on smiling, he adds, "Quit it! I mean it," he says the last part like a warning.

I want to keep on getting on his nerves, but I figure I have done enough, so I dial my grin down to a 'sensible smile.' A sensible smile is the only smile deemed okay by Clive's standards; it is an average smile that doesn't show too much teeth.

I look down at the letter again, reading it for the fifth time since I saw it on the bedside table; I sigh.

"You do know you have to tell him, right? Cade? You have to tell him about me," Clive says.

I don't look at Clive; I continue smoothing down the paper. "I know," I say under my breath.

"What was that?" Clive asks.

I bring my head up sharply, "I said I know! Okay? I know!" I practically shout at Clive.

He doesn't seem fazed; he just looks at me with bored eyes.

"Good. Because you have to, there is no future for the two of you unless you tell him," Clive says.

I twist my fingers together; I continue playing with the edge of the paper. "Well, what if-"

Clive cuts me off, "No, no 'what ifs,' at all. You have to tell him, period," I still don't bring my head up, "Olivia."

Suddenly frustrated, I jump up from the bed; with jerky movements, I put on a robe, "Argh!" I walk a few feet away from it, towards the window; I stand still for a while; my back to Clive, my shoulders hunched, and my hands in my hair. And then I whirl back, looking at Clive with desperate eyes. "Don't you get it, Clive?! I get it! I know I have to tell him, but don't you see how hard it is? Don't you see what it could mean for us? For me? All these feelings I have inside of me for him, what do I do with them? Uh? Do I just throw them away? That is not even possible; they are going to swallow me whole."

I walk slowly back towards the bed, and my eyes fixed on Clive; I stop in front of his nightstand and crouch so that I am at eye level with him.

"Once I tell him, it's over, Clive. If I tell him I betray him, and he sees everything we've had this past week, every gesture, every move, every feeling," I close my eyes, and I feel a crushing pain in my chest, "there are so many feelings, Clive," I open my eyes, "and he'll see everything as a lie."

I pause, and I take a deep breath because, at the thought of Cade seeing everything we had as a lie, breathing becomes difficult.

"It is going to crush me, Clive," I say quietly.

There is silence in the room for a while; I sit on my back legs, and my shoulders are hunched in dejection. Clive sighs.

"I hate to do this to you, but I think I'm doing it because I love you," Clive's brows furrow as he says this; Love is a strange emotion for Clive, "but I am still going to tell you that you have to tell him."

I sigh, stand up slowly, and walk towards the closet. Even though my life feels like it's slowly ending, I still have to pretend to be a human being; I have to find clothes to wear. I go through the clothes hung in the closet, but I don't really see them. All I see is grey, grey, grey. I picked out a knee-length dress; as I said, I don't know what color. I go into the bathroom to change. I come out a minute later and stand in the middle of the room, now in the dress with no color that I picked.

"And you know the worst part? My time with him- and everything we have done together- has been the most amazing part of my life, and yet it's not enough," my voice cracks, "It is nowhere near enough. Because I want more, I want so much more," I stop talking because a sob catches in my throat.

Clive clears his throat. "Well, you never know; you may still get to have it. I mean, you are mourning a relationship that is not technically over yet. You haven't even told him yet; there is no way of knowing how he would respond to it," he pauses, "'It' being a magical urn that has basically been controlling his moves and actions, birthing the uncertainty of his feelings, his lady's- your- feelings towards him, his charm, and virtually every decision he's ever made since he met you." Clive stops talking, realizing the direction his little 'pep talk' had gone.

"Oops," he says.

I stare at him for a full minute, my anxiety returning in full after Clive's not-so-reassuring talk. I run my hand through my hair again, this time scattering the previously tamed bed hair. I sit on the edge of the bed, the enormity of what is before me fully dawning on me. "What am I going to do, Clive?"

There is silence for a beat, and then Clive says, "Well, maybe if he doesn't see how great you are even after you tell him about me, or he doubts his feelings for you, then maybe he is not the right guy for you," Clive says. I know he is just trying to make me feel better.

I look at him, "I know you don't actually believe that," I say. I stand up and walk over to the closet.

"Sure, I do," Clive says, still trying to sound convincing.

I turn back to look at him, "Okay, be very honest here and say you would not be bothered if a woman you liked revealed that the first time you met her was not actually a coincidence but an event that happened because she wished it, on a magical urn." Clive looks sheepish already, but I continue, "And the first meeting wasn't the only instance in which she used the urn; no, if it was, that would have been marginally better because even though you guys meeting each other wasn't exactly coincidence, if it was just that once, every other thing that followed was your own doing. Every kiss, every feeling, every touch; you did all that, on your own."

Agitated now, I start to pace the room, "But, it wasn't just that first time; 'Remember your sick niece, yeah, you know, the one that is not so sick anymore? Yep. I did that. with my wish. On a magical urn.'" Clive looks like he wants to say something, but I cut him off and continue pacing, somehow unable to stop the flow of words now that I had started, "Oh, and that's not the end of it, 'Remember when you professed your feelings to me at the bonfire? You felt compelled, didn't you? Just like that first day when we met, and you said you felt drawn to me, yeah, remember that?'" I pause, giving Clive a meaningful look, "'Yep. Me again.' 'The mysterious condom you found in your back pocket? That was all me, baby,'" I say in a saccharine sweet tone.

I run my hands through my hair again, "How does anyone come back from that?! How do I say something like that?"

Clive has a look on his face like the one on Racheal's face that time in Friends; when Chandler was bitching about the wristwatch Joey gave him to Racheal, and Joey walks in.

"I think you just did," Cade says from behind me, but I am fervently praying to every god I know that it isn't him standing there.

Crap.

THE 'CLIVE' SECRET

I turn slowly till I come face-to-face with Cade. God, he looks even more handsome this morning. How can he look more handsome from last night? I mean, how is that even possible?

He walks slowly into the room, clutching a paper bag filled, I am sure, with chicken wings for me; my chest constricts again. I watch him watch me as he stops just a few feet away from me; his eyes are unreadable again - reminding me of that time, after the night of the bonfire, with Elena and Natalie- and even though I am not touching him, I know his whole body is tense. I can feel the tension rolling off of him in waves, and I can see the rigidity clearly from where I'm standing. He looks over at Clive on the nightstand, his brows furrow; he is trying to understand.

I start to take a step toward him, but I stop when he looks at me, with a slight warning in his eyes that I should not come closer. My fingers curl into a fist; they uncurl again, and I swallow. "Please, Cade, let me explain," I say, and my voice sounds cracked and unconvincing, even to me. I clear my throat and attempt to try again, I try to convey my love through my eyes, but it doesn't look like it's working, as Cade continues staring at me like I am a stranger. And God, that hurts. That look he's giving me like he doesn't know who I am anymore.

I steel my heart, though; now is not the time to break down, now is the time to make things right. As this thought passes through my mind, I have deja vu; I have done this before; the morning after the bonfire, I had also had to steel my heart, even though it was breaking, to try to make things right. Funny how the two events suddenly have so much in common. Except, I remember when I tried to make things better with that situation, I blamed it on the alcohol. There is no alcohol involved here.

So, I just have to end this the way I started it, with the truth.

"Cade, I know you are upset right now, given what you just heard," I am buoyed by how stable my voice manages to sound, and that gives me the courage to continue, "but I assure you that all your feelings and actions up till this moment, have all been purely yours."

My newfound confidence shakes, though, when Cade's eyes narrow. I should not have led with that. Stupid, stupid, stupid.

I try again, "I know you must have questions-"

Cade cuts me off, "You know? Are you sure you know? Cause I don't think you do," he drops the paper bag he is holding on the nightstand and starts walking towards me, "I come in, thinking I'd meet my girlfriend waiting for me on the bed, or in the shower, or, hell, on the desk. Believe me; I let my imagination run wild there. But, instead, what do I walk into? You talking to-," he breaks off here to look at Clive, he looks back at me, even more confused, "yourself," he says, "Or is it.... that?" he asks me, pointing at Clive.

"Okay, bucko, I am not a 'thing,'" Clive says, with enough indignation that I steal a glance at him.

Cade catches my glance; he looks from me to Clive, "Well? Are you talking to an urn, Olivia?" Cade's voice is starting to sound hysterical now.

"Okay, seriously, what is this guy's deal? Is it so weird that somebody would be talking to an urn?" Clive says.

I close my eyes, unable to believe what I am hearing, unable to believe the situation that I put myself in. How do you tell your boyfriend that 'Yes, indeed, I have been talking to an urn'? But I look into Cade's eyes, and I know I have no choice. He looks very determined to get answers, and besides, he deserves the truth.

I breathe in deeply and look Cade directly in his eyes. We have always been straight with each other, except for admitting how we felt about each other from the beginning. We have never kept a secret from each other, right from the beginning of the trip. And even with our feelings, even though we never said it out loud, it was always in our eyes. The point is, we have been straight with each other, and that is a very good quality, a quality I want to keep going.

"Yes, the urn talks," I say, pointing to Clive, "his name is Clive."

"Hi," Clive says.

And then I proceed to tell Cade everything.

***

Twenty minutes later, I am seated on the edge of the bed, Cade on the wooden stool at the far side of the room. We are adjacent to each other, and the room is not so big that the distance between us is that wide, but I feel like Cade is an ocean away from me. I could feel him withdrawing as I told the story of Clive, how he came into my life, his influence on our time together, and the decisions we made.

He wrings his hands together, saying nothing. I stare at him, also saying nothing.

"Wow, it's like *Sophie's Choice*," Clive says, his voice hushed in the quiet room.

It is like *Sophie's Choice*; there is no good outcome to this. I knew it before I told him; I knew telling him would change things between us, but I still did. I'm sure I had a good reason for going ahead with telling him, but right now, watching him trying to process everything I just told him and not knowing what the next words that are going to come out of his mouth are going to be, I suddenly cannot remember what those good reasons were.

This is my life here, I found something good with Cade, something amazing, and now it might all be taken away from me. In the blink of an eye, it could all be gone. A lump forms in my throat, and I try to swallow, but it is too big to go through, so it just sits there. I know what I can do to make this all go away. I look at Clive; after a minute of staring at him, he catches on to me. He doesn't shake his head or tell me not to do it; he just looks right back at me. I smile wryly; I guess it's not only Cade who knows me so well.

I could wish this all away, this moment right here, this torturous moment after telling Cade the truth and waiting for his response, I could wish it all away, and it would all vanish like it never happened, but I can't. What I have with Cade is something special, and the only stain on it is *this* secret. And so, even though it is currently driving a mile-wide wedge between us, I will not take the easy way out. I want everything with Cade, and I will not allow a secret to get in the way of that. I deserve that much. Cade deserves that and more.

So, I'm seated, with a lump too big to swallow, in my throat, waiting for Cade's next words, the words that will either break me or give me hope. When I cannot take it anymore, I am about to say something when Cade clears his throat.

I look up sharply, and I meet Cade's eyes looking steadily at me; and they are unreadable, but they are focused on me. He says quietly, and with pain that breaks my heart all the way, "You can wish this moment away, can't you?"

I close my eyes; I feel the tears forming. I open them and look at him as directly as he did me, "I can. But I won't," I say, my voice cracking at the end.

Cade nods. "Why not?" he asks.

I am surprised by his question because this is not at all how I expected this to go. "I, I'm not sure, I just-" I break off my sentence because I don't know what else to say. I am at a loss of what to say to that question, 'why not?' like a plea; it was like he was begging me to do it. I look into his eyes, and finally, I am able to read them. He has let his guard down, and now with pain, betrayal, and doubt, I see fear and pleading.

My own eyes well with tears again, and this time, I let them flow. "Cade, I-," I try to say something, anything, to let him know I would do anything to erase this moment right now if it wouldn't hurt him or our future's chances of being together without blemish.

Clive is like an illegitimate child, borne by me, or an illicit affair, or a wound, and as long as we don't get honest about him, he will continue to fester. I will keep on having that nagging feeling of not telling Cade the whole truth about how we met, the night of the bonfire, and his niece; Kayla, and one day, the weight of the kept secret will come crashing down on me, and I will lose it, and probably destroy a lot more than our relationship, when I do.

Cade clears his throat again. "You know what, forget I said that. So, that day, when I helped you fix your car, and I told you I felt drawn to you, you knew what it meant?"

I nod, and I was going to leave it at that because I don't trust my own voice right now, but as always, what Cade deserves outweighs my own inconvenience, so I say, "Yes, I knew why you felt drawn was because I wished for you."

Cade nods, and I see the muscle in his jaw tick. "So, if it wasn't for your wish, we never would have met."

This is it; this is the moment of truth, the origin of the whole issue. This is the moment that determines how our whole relationship is viewed by Cade, and it breaks my heart that I have no better explanation for it because, for all intents and purposes, we would never have met. I am a believer in fate and destiny, and I believe some people are meant to meet in their lifetime, to either fall in love, be best of friends, or even business partners. I truly believe there are people who are meant for one another. But even I cannot apply that here because Clive being a factor makes the whole theory null and void. Clive is real; the wishes are too, so the idea that we would have met regardless doesn't stand anymore.

So, all I can say to Cade's question is, "Yes," even if it breaks my heart.

Cade nods again and stands up, but he doesn't look at me as he says, "I need some air."

I stand too, aching to go to him but remaining where I am because I understand that for now, this is my place.

When he gets to the door, he stops, and without turning, he says quietly, "Thank you for Kayla."

And then he opens the door, and leaves, taking my shattered heart with him.

REFLECTIONS

It's been an hour since Cade left, and I am going crazy; the cozy hotel room feels bigger than it actually is, and the silence is deafening.

"Where do you think he is, Clive?" I ask, probably for the hundredth time. I chew my nails, and then I realize what I am doing, and I stop. God, I'm a mess.

Clive sighs; for the hundredth time too. "I do not know, Olivia. I am not a magical urn that can tell where people are," he says dryly, rolling his eyes at me.

I sigh too. "I'm sorry, Clive, I'm sorry," I say, sitting on the bed, resigned.

"It's okay," Clive assures me.

My eyes stray to the TV in the room, and I see the highlights of the news and the weather, it says that the roads are free, the skies are clear, and it would be a good day to travel. As I see this, my heart does a painful thump because I know what good weather and free roads meant for Cade and me; nothing good. Nothing is stopping Cade from packing up and leaving right now, which I wouldn't really blame him for, I mean, one; he must really miss his niece; Kayla, and especially now that she is healed, he would want to see more than ever, and two; the situation between us is kind of awkward and weird right now. So, there's not really a very valid reason for him to stay. Oh, and third, I bet time away from me would seem like a pretty good idea right about now.

I cover my face with my hands and groan into them. "Argh! Everything's all messed up. I messed everything up," I say, in kind of like a whisper to myself.

But of course, Clive hears it, and his response to it is, "Yep, you did."

I don't reply to him because I barely hear him; I am thinking of how great it would be if Cade would just come back to the room so we could talk about everything. What telling him about Clive means to our relationship, how it has changed our status and the way forward. Does he even want to go forward? Did the secret change too much for him? What is he thinking? All these thoughts run through my head, and it is really frustrating not to know the answers.

I imagine what it would be like if we had more time if Cade didn't decide to take advantage of the clear skies to leave early, but instead, he stays, and we talk about everything he's thinking. I clear my mind and imagine just the two of us talking, and that's all I am thinking about as I say quietly to myself, "I wish we had more time."

My hands are still on my face, and I stay this way for another minute, and then I bring my head up. I look at Clive, and he is looking at me in a weird way.

"What?" I ask when he doesn't say anything and just continues to stare at me.

He looks at me, and in a calm tone, he says, "You just made a wish."

"What? No, I didn't," I automatically say because I didn't make a wish. I didn't.

"Yes, you did," Clive insists.

"When?" I ask

"Just now," Clive says, eerily calm in a way that I would normally have overlooked but that, at this point in time, I find infuriating.

"Okay, would you stop that?!" I snap at him.

"What?" he says, trying to look innocent. Oh, he knows what he's doing.

I kneel down on the room floor, in front of the nightstand, putting my eyes directly at Clive's eye level; through gritted teeth, I ground out, "Explain."

My seriousness must have gotten through cause he stopped yanking my chain, "Well, just earlier, you said you wish you and Cade had more time."

"Yeah?"

"And I guess your mind must have been clear because I felt the wish leave me as you said the words."

"You felt the wish 'leave you?'" I ask, incredulous, a part of me still finding it hard to believe that I may have just used my last wish, and I hadn't even known.

Clive sighs, "Yeah, well, you see, I have never really explained how the wish thing works to you, have I?"

"No," I say.

"Well, it's not mandatory I do, so it must have slipped my mind," Clive says nonchalantly.

I rub a hand on my forehead; a headache is starting to brew. "So, what you're telling me right now is that you have no control whatsoever on how the wish gets out because the wishes just 'leave you.' Is that it?"

"Yes, that is correct."

I close my eyes and pinch the bridge of my nose. "And I have just made my last wish, meaning I have no wish left," I pause, having to swallow past the ball of dread I can now taste in my throat before I add, "Am I right?"

Clive, too pauses a beat before he answers.

"Yes," he says.

"Oh, God," I say, the enormity of the whole thing finally catching up to me, "Oh, God," I say again. "What am I going to do?!"

I turn desperate eyes on Clive.

"Well, on the bright side, it's not a completely bad wish. If you really think about it, it's a perfect wish, considering the situation you and Cade are in, and that time is, in fact, what you both need right now."

"Yeah, but have you forgotten the reason for the whole 'situation'?!" I exclaim as I stand up from the bed and start pacing the room, "The whole reason why there is a 'situation' is because of making wishes in the first place. I mean, don't you see what this means?!"

"Okay, well, relax, alright," Clive says.

I whirl on him, "Relax?! Relax, did you say? I should 'relax' when I am in such a major stitch, I just made a massive mistake, and you're telling me to relax?"

Clive gives me a dry look, "Okay, don't yell at me. I'm not the one who made the wish."

I sigh, exasperated. I turn to the TV again, and this time the headline on the news says there is a storm rolling in; they don't know where it came from; it's like it's coming out of nowhere, and it is huge. They advise people not to go out in it.

"The wish is in effect," Clive says from behind me.

I hang my head for a minute, and then I bring it up back, having made up my mind.

"I have to tell Cade," I say.

"You have to tell Cade what?" Clive asks.

I turn to face Clive; my face is resolute. "I have to tell him that I made another wish," I say.

Clive's eyebrows come up, "Do you think that's a good idea? He might not take it so well."

"Well, regardless. I am not going to keep this a secret from him, not again."

Clive doesn't say anything at first; he just looks at me and says, "Think about it very carefully, Olivia; he might be wrapping his mind around the whole thing already, you know, gradually being okay with it, and, if you tell him this now, it could ruin all that. He might not be able to come back from it this time, and that would be the end of it for both of you."

The lump in my throat swells at Clive's words because I know he is only giving me cold, hard facts, a look into a very real possibility. But even as I think about his words, even as I consider not telling Cade and just hoping that everything works out well in the end, I already know I am not going to keep it a secret from him. First of all, keeping secrets was what got us into this mess in the first place; second of all, he deserves the truth and nothing but. Third, and probably the most gut-wrenching of all, I probably have nothing to lose. He probably, right now, is still not wrapping his head around the whole thing and is considering ending it all, so I might as well go all in.

I pick up my phone from the nightstand and dial his number, it goes through, but he doesn't pick up. See? Nothing to lose. My chest constricts painfully as I dial again; still no response.

"Maybe it's a sign," Clive says quietly from behind me, on the nightstand.

No, it's not a sign, it's an easy way out, and even though it pains me, I am not going to take it. I dial his number again and wait for the beep. I leave a message.

CADE

Olivia's voice filters through my phone speaker, and I close my eyes at the sound of it. God, it physically pains me to hear her voice. Her voice, for God's sake. With difficulty, I try to focus on what she's saying, and I feel my body tense up as I listen. She made another wish.

I open my eyes and throw my head back to look up at the open sky above me. It just keeps getting crazier, doesn't it? After Olivia had told me about the- it still feels weird to even think it- magical urn, and the wishes, and how we met not being a coincidence, I had needed space, and time to myself, to really digest what she said and to analyze how I felt about the whole thing. I had left the hotel room, not knowing where I was going to go per se. My plan had been to just keep on walking till I got to someplace, but when I got to the lobby, I realized the plan was a stupid one- I could get lost- and so I asked the receptionist at the front desk where she could recommend to me that was quiet and peaceful. I told her I needed to think, and she described where I currently am to me. It is a garden of sorts, Jane- the receptionist- had told me it belonged to the owner, but she uses it more than him ever since she stumbled on it accidentally a few weeks ago. I had thanked her for sharing her secret hideout with me, and I had come here, although looking at the way the structure of the 'garden' was built; high ceilings, and transparent glass walls, it looked more like a greenhouse to me. But it is quiet, and that's all I need.

And so, for the past hour, I have been going back and forth on what Olivia told me, and, naturally, the whole thing is all undeniably weird and makes me feel doubtful of the past week. I remember the way Olivia looks at me whenever that sizzling thing that always happens between us starts. I know how she responded to me when we had sex; I know I made her tremble. I felt her tremble in my arms. Nobody was that good an actor, and even if she was, Olivia is not a phony. This I know with certainty.

Even in light of the revealed secret, I know Olivia is not a liar. And she didn't fake those feelings.

How we met wasn't a coincidence; she pulled me to her, the night at the bonfire; she compelled me to confess my feelings. I am not sure how I feel about these two things because they were both done against my will, but I might as well not be a hypocrite and say I mind how it all turned out. This past week has been the best week of my life, and if there is something I absolutely believe in, it's the fragility of life. I am not going to tie it down in doubts; I refuse to.

And she healed Kayla. That is not something I can even begin to quantify.

So, now, as I listen to her confess, with tears and fear thick in her voice, to something that obviously doesn't help matters- but still she does it anyway- I know it doesn't matter.

No wish made me fall in love with Olivia Henson. It was all her.

ENDINGS AND BEGINNINGS

The windows rattle with the force of the wind; I walk over and close them. I turn to Clive and throw my hands up in exasperation. "You couldn't have thought of a safer way to give us more time?!"

"Hey, don't look at me; I don't make the rules," Clive says, clearly unbothered by the raging madness of the blizzard going on outside.

I roll my eyes and walk over to the sofa on the opposite end of the room; I flop down on it and sigh heavily. I check my phone for the hundredth time; still nothing. I groan loudly.

"You know, groaning and sighing have not been certified as surefire methods of making someone appear," I lift my head and look at Clive, "researchers have said," he finishes lamely. I stare at him, shooting daggers at him through my eyes; when he just stares owlishly back, I just sigh and throw my head back on the sofa's headrest.

"Why won't he call?" I whine, and before Clive can say anything, which, even though I don't lift my head up from the sofa again, I know what he is about to say, and I know it is not going to be helpful, I add, "Don't even say anything."

There is silence in the room for a while, and then Clive breaks it.

"You know, just as a way of distracting you from waiting for Cade's call, this will probably be the last time we're together. Just the two of us." I lift my head up slowly from the couch and look towards Clive. He continues, "So, I don't know, maybe we ought to say our goodbyes."

I stare at him for a full minute, and then I say, "Oh."

"Look, it's not a big deal; we don't have to do it. I don't want to do it; it's just that some other people I had been assigned to made a big show of it or got a big kick out of it." I'm still staring at him as he continues talking. I'm just finding it hard to believe that I really have to say goodbye now. Until Clive said it, I hadn't really thought about saying goodbye, but I guess I should have. Clive is still talking, "But, you know, if you don't want to do it, that's fine too," he says.

"No, no, I want to do it," I say. I definitely want to say goodbye to Clive, "But does it have to be now? I mean, do you have to leave now?"

"Well, I'm not leaving right this second," Clive says.

"No, I know, I know. But you are leaving today, aren't you?" I ask, part of me already knowing the answer.

"Yes, I am," Clive says, "You just used your last wish, and this is the seventh day we've been together. For all intents and purposes, our time together is at an end."

"Wow. Seven days." I shake my head, smiling at Clive, "Feels like an eternity since SpellBound's book launch party."

"Yeah," Clive says, smiling too, "You were a young, dreamy-eyed secretary with a broken heart from a douche king that was beneath her anyway; now, look at you all grown up, heart full, and focused on bigger things than revenge on an asshole."

Clive finishes his summary of my life in the past seven days with a dry tone, and what an acute summary, I think to myself.

I laugh, "Yeah, I'm all grown up now," I say, my tone falling as my thoughts stray to Cade again. I don't feel grown up; I just feel apprehensive.

"Hey," I turn to meet Clive's eyes; they are focused on me and very serious as he says, "You are grown up. I've watched you grow up right in front of me with my own two eyes. And even though you think Cade is the reason for all the positive changes in your life right now- because I know that's what you're thinking- he's not. Yes, Cade has been a very vital and positive factor in your life these past few days, but you also get to take credit for opening up your heart to said positive changes. You allowed yourself to let go of the past, opened yourself up to discussing the deeply buried pain of the loss of your parents, and took the very courageous step of falling in love. Yeah, I know they say that falling in love is not a choice and that 'it just happens,' but I truly believe human beings have the strength not to succumb to it. And that's the really courageous part of falling in love, subjecting yourself to that vulnerability. And you did that. and I am proud of you for it. No matter what happens between you and Cade from here on out, know that you're better off for loving him at all."

I quickly wipe away the tears already streaming down my face.

"Oh, man," I say tearfully.

"Oh, man," Clive says disgruntledly.

But after his speech, I don't believe his flippantness anymore. I smile, "Oh, hush, you love me," I say, happy to be able to rib him. Clive just rolls his eyes. Then something occurs to me, "God, I didn't think of anything to say to you; I never thought I'd have to say it so soon."

Clive shrugs, "It's cool, really. You don't have to say anything; really, I wouldn't want you going all mushy on me again."

"No, no way, I have to say something. We can't part ways without me saying something," I say.

"Well, geez, you would think I was dying or something."

"Well, you are going away," I say.

Clive rolls his eyes again and sighs, "Fine then. Just make it quick; I don't want any sappy lines either; well, you're the writer."

"You're right," I say as I smile and move closer to the nightstand; I crouch in front of Clive and look at his reflection on the surface of the urn. I smile, "I am a writer, and being that, it gives me an insight into things and people, it helps me see things that other people normally wouldn't see, which is why, behind that hard exterior and front you put on- literally and figuratively- I know that you are a caring soul, a magical being who is not only magical because of your ability to grant wishes but also magical because of your innate care for the people you are put in charge of. You don't have to care for us, you didn't have to care for me when I was nervous about the book launch party at SpellBounds', all you had to do was grant me my wish, and you had already done that before the party. But you did, and you helped me pick out my dress, and you helped me through the event with what you said to me before the party. You didn't have to care for Lane Kim when she was being intimidated by those mean girls in her school, but you did."

"All right, all right, I get it; I'm a softie," Clive says, cutting me off.

I laugh and softly caress the urn at its sides, "Yes, you are," I say.

Clive rolls his eyes, but after a while, he also laughs.

Just then, Cade enters the room.

"A strange man just waved at me in the lobby, he smiled at me, and I don't even know him. Weird," Cade says.

The light mood in the room vanishes, the smile on my face melts away, and I feel the tension come back into my body as I look up at him, at his unreadable face, my hands still holding Clive. Cade's eyes flick to the urn; I look down too and remove my hand quickly as if it burns. Cade looks away from the urn, his face still unreadable, and looks at me. My heart gallops as I look into his silver-grey eyes; will I never see them again?

Cade inclines his head slightly towards a corner on the far side of the room, "Can I talk to you for a minute?" he asks quietly.

"Sure," I say, standing up from my position on the floor. My hands feel clammy; I don't even sweat that much.

I walk over to the corner with Cade, and we face each other. I should probably apologize again, I think to myself, but I know that at this point, Cade's already made his choice. He wouldn't have come back otherwise.

He rubs a hand over his forehead, and I see a hint of fatigue on his face. My heart sinks even further.

"I'm sorry I didn't pick up your call or send you a message. I just really needed the time to myself, and I didn't want anything to interfere with that," Cade says.

My heart constricts even more at his words. Cade is the type of guy who would first apologize for not returning calls before saying anything else, and that makes me realize all the more that I don't want to lose a guy that is as good as Cade.

Because Cade is looking at me, obviously expecting a response to his apology, I clear my throat and focus on the present. "It's okay," I say, forcing the words out of my mouth, past the lump in my throat.

He nods, his head bent, and then he looks into my eyes, and as he starts talking, the tiny little hope that I had been stamping down on for the past hour starts to spring back to life.

"Look, Olivia, I don't want to let you go, not now, not ever. I know we never talked about future plans or goals, but ever since I said 'I love you,' I brandished all thoughts of breaking up or letting you go. And although I never imagined there would be this kind of secret between us and that it would come to light, I was pretty sure of my feelings for you and of where I saw us going. And now that the secret's out, and I know everything," he cuts off, "I do know everything, right?"

With tears in my eyes, and lumps clogging my throat, I nod my head and manage to push out, "Yeah, you know everything."

Cade nods. "Now that I know everything- and although it took me, God, one hour, to think about it all and come to terms with everything; the urn, the magic, the wishes, the ripple effects of it all on our relationship, and, yes, the doubts now, cause there will always be doubts, I don't think there's a way around that- I am now more sure than ever that I want to spend the rest of my life with you. I want you, Olivia Henson, magical urns, wishes, not-so-coincidental first meetings, now and forever." He takes a deep breath here; the air is now charged again between us; he continues, "I'm wearing my heart on my sleeve here. Will you take me?"

I look into the eyes of the man before me, the man I love, the man whose heart is already so big for forgiving me, and yet is the one still asking if I'd take him. If I'd take him? Will I ever?!

I jump on Cade; he lets out a soft 'oomph' as he catches me.

UNCLE JASPER

"Okay, so how does this work?" Cade asks, forty-five minutes later, after the best moment of my life.

I look sideways at him; we're both seated on the sofa, arms linked, and I stare at his beautiful face.

"Olivia?"

"Earth to Cinder-livia," Clive says dryly.

I snap back to the conversation. "Uh?" I say, looking from Cade to Clive.

"He asks how it all works, dummy," Clive says.

I turn to Cade, "How what works?"

The blizzard is still going crazy outside; the windows rattle in tune with the wind's sound. While it had been a useful tactic that had kept us together, giving us the time we both needed to talk about Clive and all the wishes I had made- something we had talked about in length after Cade had said he wanted to spend the rest of his life with me- now I just want the blizzard to stop, so Cade and I can check out of the hotel, and start our life together, outside, in the real world.

We haven't talked about all of that yet, but I know Cade would want to go home as soon as possible; he would want to see Kayla with his own two eyes and hug her tight. And I will follow him if he lets me- which I have a very strong feeling he would- I want to meet the angelic Kayla myself and hug her tight too. I want to meet the rest of his family, his sisters, his mother, and his cousins. Now that I'm all alone in the sense that I have no blood relatives meeting a big family like Cades' has me excited.

"Well, about how Clive gets handed to the next person," Cade says in response to my question.

"Oh. Yeah, we were talking about that just before you came in," I say as I turn to Clive, "Who's Uncle Jasper?" I ask.

"I can't tell you that."

"Still?!" I say. Remembering when Clive first got dropped off at my doorstep, he said he couldn't tell me who Uncle Jasper was. "But, you're leaving already; I mean, how do I know who to hand you off to?"

"Don't worry about handing me off to Uncle Jasper, just focus on finding the next person to get seven wishes."

"Wait, I have to pick the next person?!" I exclaim; this is the first time I'm hearing of this.

Clive looks sheepish, "I didn't tell you?"

"No, you didn't!"

"Oops," Clive says.

"Okay, what is going on? I can only hear your side of the conversation," Cade says, looking between Clive and me.

I turn to Cade, "Sorry, I forgot you couldn't hear him. He's just now telling me that I have to be the one to pick out his next recipient."

"Oh. Well, did he say what would happen if you didn't get anyone?" Cade asks.

"No, no, he didn't say," I reply, already feeling stressed out by the responsibility of finding someone new for Clive.

"Okay, let's take this step by step, then. First, we find out who Uncle Jasper is. Finding out who he is- and I can't believe I'm going to say this, seeing as 'Uncle Jasper' is a mythical unknown character- is more realistic than just finding a random person who must also be worthy of having Clive. What do you think?"

"You should listen to him; he's really making a lot of sense. Are you sure he hasn't done this before?" Clive asks, giving Cade a suspicious look.

I just give Clive a look and turn back to Cade. "Yeah, I think that sounds like a great idea," I say.

"Yeah? Okay, let's get started then. Do you remember anything from the first day Clive got dropped off?"

I think back to the day in question, "Yeah, I remember the delivery guy, he was really surly and moody, probably cause it was a Monday morning, and he had been at my door for a while before I answered him. Anyway, uh, I think that was all I saw," I say, not really remembering anything worth anything about that day.

"We need more than that. Think harder, any phone number, logo, or company name on the delivery guy's shirt?"

Something starts to trickle into my memory. "Wait, I think I remember something. The delivery guy was covering the truck mostly, so I couldn't really get a good look at it-"

"What truck?" Cade asks.

I rack my brain, "Uh, the truck he used to deliver the package; it was a brown truck, I remember that and it had a logo, or icon, of some sort, like an infinity sign, but with a crack at its side."

"Okay, can you draw it?" Cade asks me

I nod, "Yeah, I can try."

Cade picks up his laptop from the bed and opens a recognition software app on it. I try to draw what I remember from the logo on the app's PowerPoint software, Cade runs it through, and it brings out a list of possible companies with the logo. We see dry cleaning services, office supply companies, restaurants, and finally, one delivery company, Ricky's.

"Ricky's?" I say out loud, "What does that have to do with anything?"

Cade clicks on the delivery company's icon, and it brings up information about the company. The staff, their delivery time, their jurisdiction; my home address is an hour's drive from their office. Cade keeps on scrolling through.

"What are you looking for?" I ask him.

"Pictures of the employees, hopefully, a group photo," as he says this, a group picture with the heading 'Staff of '01' pops up. Cade clicks on it.

"Does anyone look familiar?" he asks me.

I look at the employees' faces, one after the other, "No, I don't. The delivery guy isn't there. Where did he come from?"

Cade is still staring intently at the screen, and then suddenly, he points at the janitor, an old man at the far end of the picture. "I've seen this man before," Cade says.

"Where?" I ask.

Cade's face scrunches up in thought, and then he lights up as he remembers, "He was the man I told you about, the one who waved at me in the lobby," Cade says, already standing up from his chair. I follow him picking up Clive on my way out.

"Wow," Clive says, under my arm.

***

While Cade scans the lobby area for the man he saw earlier, I sight a commotion happening a few feet away from where we are standing. I walk towards the people there, and I see a man dressed in a suit, who I assume is the hotel manager, as he is the one trying to calm another man down. This man is six feet tall, a shadow of a beard on his chin, and his dark brown hair all ruffled up like he had been running his hand through it. His face is turned away from me, but even from where I'm standing, behind him, I can feel the agitation coming off him in waves, and then he turns, running his hand through his hair again, and throwing his head back in frustration, and I see his eyes. His eyes are so full of pain, and my heart constricts just looking at them. In addition to the agitation he is feeling right now because of whatever it is the hotel manager is saying, there is a deep past pain in his eyes, and it is so great and heavy, and I don't know how I know this, maybe because I recognize it from when I looked in the mirror a week after my parents died, but I just know that this man's pain had to do with death.

"I'm telling you, my daughter is in the hospital; she had an asthma attack; I need to get to her," the man says, energy rippling through his arms, the only thing stopping him from bolting through the doors of the hotel and into the raging blizzard were the two burly security guards holding both his arms.

"And I'm telling you, Mr. Lawson, that you can't go into that blizzard. You're going to die in that thing!" the hotel manager says.

"I don't care!" Mr. Lawson shouts back at the hotel manager.

They continued arguing, but I tuned them out because I already got what was happening. When I made a wish to give Cade and me more time and a second chance at our love, I indirectly trapped a man- who had already lost someone- in a hotel, keeping him from being with someone else that he cared about so very deeply.

While the feeling of sick guilt washes through me, Cade walks over to me.

"I found him; I found the man who was waving at me. He's sitting on one of the lobby chairs, and though our eyes didn't meet, I know he saw me. I think he's waiting for you, Olivia," Cade says.

I take one last look at Mr. Lawson and then turn to Cade, "I think I've found the next recipient too."

"You have?" Cade asks.

I nod. "Yeah. Let's go meet Uncle Jasper," I say.

Cade nods and leads me towards a lobby chair, where an older man sits; he looks like he could be in his late fifties. He looks normal at first glance; grey hair, wrinkles on his face and hands, a gentle and calm air around him, but when you look past the physical appearance and into his dark, almost endless eyes, you know this is not a regular old man.

He smiles, and I automatically smile back.

"Olivia Henson, nice to meet you. Again."

I don't say anything because what do you say to a man you are ninety-eight percent sure is not human but a magical urn keeper who is, by all intents and purposes, a fairy god...uncle?

'Uncle Jasper' looks at Clive, who is still under my armpit, and though they don't say anything, I feel like I have passed a test when he looks back at me and smiles.

"Seems like you made good use of your seven wishes, which were really second chances, seven times. So, I believe you have picked out the next recipient?"

For the first time since meeting the mysterious Uncle Jasper, I say, "Yes, I have."

When we stare at each other and nobody makes a move, I say, "I assume you already know who it is?"

He smiles that serene smile of his again, "Yes, I do," he replies.

I nod. "Okay. Then I guess my job here is done." I place Clive in front of me; I smile at him, "I'm going to miss you," I say, and strangely, I don't feel like crying. But then again, it's probably not so strange, Clive was- like Uncle Jasper so wisely put it- my second chance, seven times over, and I am grateful for every moment.

"I'll miss you too, kiddo," Clive says and smiles too.

I smile again, and then I finally hand him over to Uncle Jasper.

"Thank you," I say, addressing Uncle Jasper. He is this mysterious person that I wouldn't know from Adam, but who just gave me the biggest chance of my life and is not even asking for anything back. Thank you is the least and yet the most expressive phrase I can say to him.

And he seems to get that because he smiles too and says, "You're welcome." He starts to leave, and then he turns back, "Your mom and dad say hello," he says, and finally walks away.

Tears well up in my eyes, and I turn to Cade, stunned, to see if he heard what Uncle Jasper just said.

"Did he just…." Cade trails off, looking confused and awed.

"He definitely did," I say, smiling through the tears. I wrap my arm around Cade's waist and turn him around to head back to our room.

MR. LAWSON

These idiots have no idea what they're doing to me. I already lost Jessica; I will NOT lose my baby girl. I calmed myself enough that the manager and his goons let me go, and while they weren't looking, I managed to rush out of the hotel into my car, and this piece of junk just won't start.

I reenter the lobby and sit in one of the armchairs trying to figure out what I can do. There's no way a cab is coming out in this to pick me up. Suddenly there is a tap on my shoulder; I turn expecting to see the manager, but instead, there's a man I've never seen before, and yet he looks so familiar.

"What is it?" I ask, annoyed that he's interrupted my train of thought.

"I believe this is yours now," he says, holding up an old urn.

"I think you're mistaken. Look, I don't have time for this. I have to figure out how to get to my little girl."

"This can help you with that," he says, with a familiar twinkle.

"Well, unless that thing can stop this storm and start my car…." I trail off as the man begins to chuckle. "What's so funny?"

"All you have to do is say 'I wish' before all of that, and you're off." He places the urn on the coffee table in front of me and steps back.

This guy is crazy, I think as I look from him to the urn.

"If I wish on this thing, you'll leave me alone?" I ask, trying to hold back my rising anger.

"Yup," he says with a smirk.

"Ok. I wish the storm would stop and my car would start so I could get to the hospital," I say.

"Sounds good to me," says a voice that seems to come from the urn itself.

It must be the strange man, probably throwing his voice like a ventriloquist. I turn to tell him he can have his urn back. I look around, and he is nowhere to be seen. I stand up and look around the lobby, when my eyes stop at the front door. The storm is gone, and the sun is out as if it hadn't been there at all.

If you liked this book

Find our fiction below!

https://www.ttpublishinghouse.com/legendsreborn

https://www.ttpublishinghouse.com/7wishes

https://www.ttpublishinghouse.com/mallcadet

Social Media

Facebook: tlmpublishinghouse

Website: www.TTpublishinghouse.com